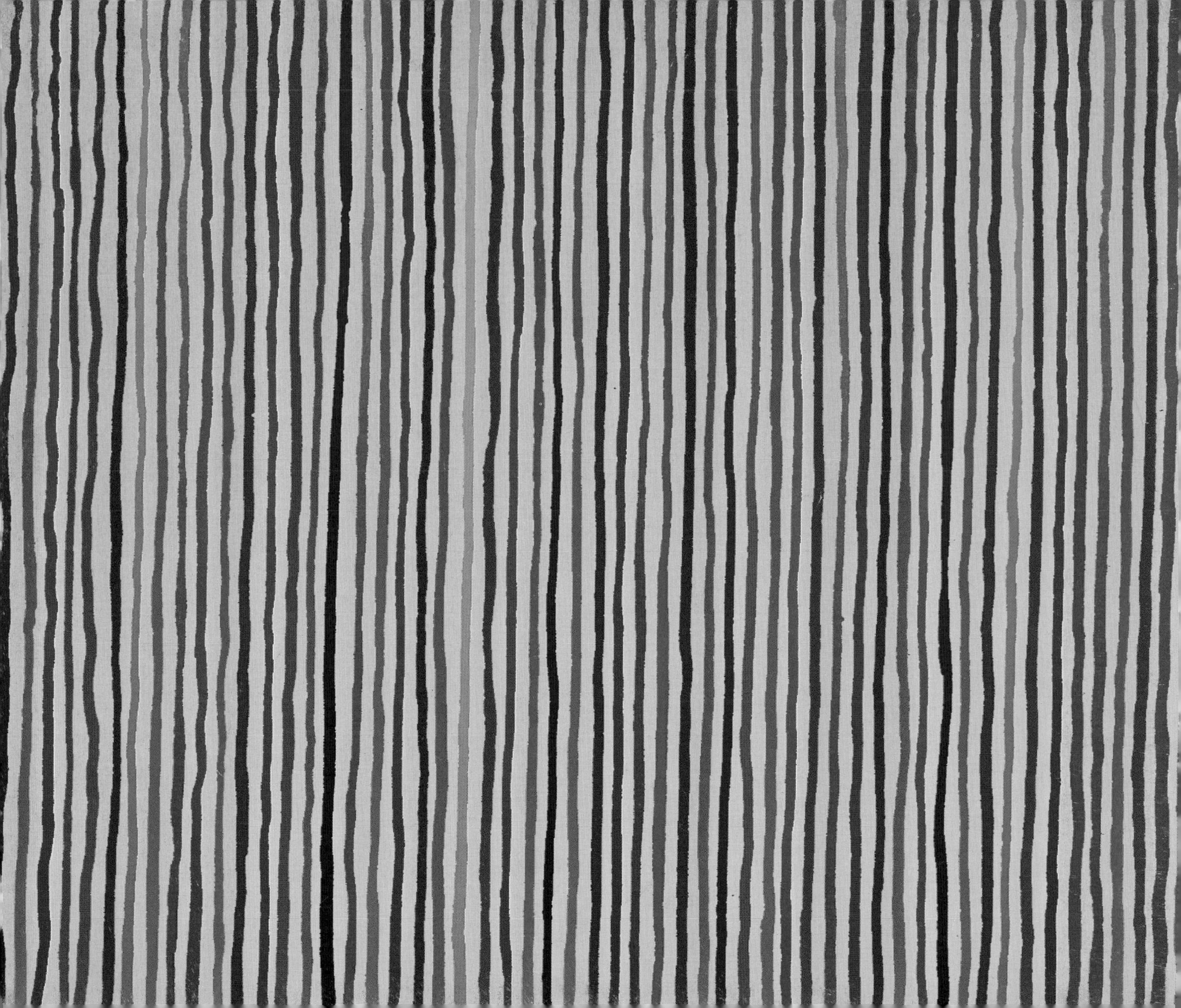

Little Baby Bobby

by Nancy Van Laan
illustrated by Laura Cornell

ALFRED A. KNOPF  New York

ALFRED A. KNOPF, INC.

http://www.randomhouse.com/

Library of Congress Cataloging-in-Publication Data
Van Laan, Nancy.
Little baby Bobby / by Nancy Van Laan ; illustrated by Laura Cornell
p.   cm.
Summary: When a bouncy baby's buggy goes whooshing down a hill, he is in
for quite a ride as an assortment of people give chase.
ISBN 0-679-84922-X   (trade)
ISBN 0-679-94922-4 (lib. bdg.)
[1. Babies—Fiction. 2. Stories in rhyme.]
I. Cornell, Laura, ill.   II. Title.
PZ8.3.V34Li   1997
[E]—dc20   94-45093
Printed in the United States of America

10 9 8 7 6 5 4 3 2 1

For Anna, my youngest and toughest critic.

—N.V.L.

For Anne.

—L.C.

Little baby Bobby
lives on a hill.
Oopsa! Oopsa!
He never sits still.
Whoosh! goes Bobby's baby buggy
down, down the hill.

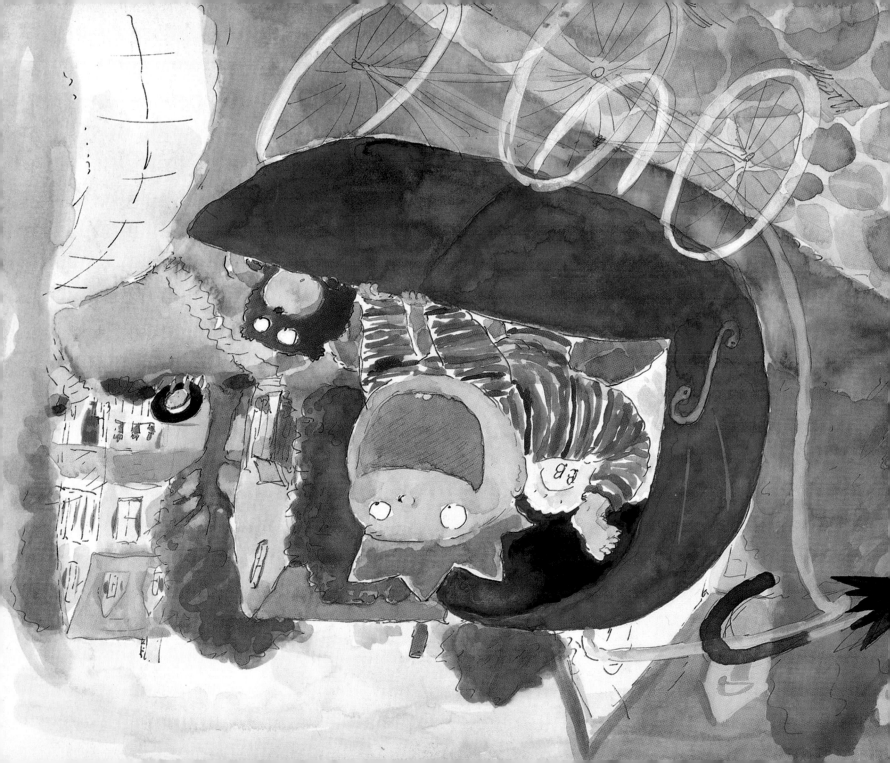

Britta, Bobby's baby-sitter,
shrieks in dismay,
"Ai-yi-yi, Yi-yi-yi!
He's runnin' clean away!"
Ker-lump! go her galoshes
as the buggy zips astray.

Little baby Bobby
babbles in delight.
Clap! go his hands
as his buggy takes flight.
"Bobby go bye-bye!"
Zoom—out of sight!

Officer Bratsky
strolls down the street.
Swoosh! goes the buggy
between his big feet.
"Stop!" yells Bratsky,
landing on his seat.

Britta chases Bobby,
with Bratsky on their tail.
Buggy hits a hydrant—*Klunk!*
Bobby needs a pail.
"*Ai-yi-yi!*" shrieks Britta.
"You'll land us all in jail."

Paddy Pig, the pretzel man,
is peddling his wares.
Smasha-crasha-smoosha!
Pretzels everywhere.
"Mmm!" coos Bobby,
and feeds his stuffed bear.

Painter Moe is busy
sprucing up the town.
Bump! goes the buggy,
and Moe tumbles down!
"Pretty!" cries Bobby.
"Britta pink and brown!"

Bouncing past Buster dog,
Bobby reaches out.
Buster chases Bobby.
Bobby pats his snout.
Grrr! growls Buster
as he bumpy-bumps about.

Britta pulls on Buster.
Flap-a-flap! They sail!
Buster chews the handle.
Britta holds his tail.
Watch out, Nicky Postman!
Away flies the mail.

"Yikes!" shouts Doctor Snide,
tossed up high.
He plops into the buggy
for a hairy-scary ride!
Maggie Baggins grabs her cats,
then tries to step aside.
But in the buggy Maggie goes,
on top of Doctor Snide!

Ta-ta-dee-dah!
The parade has begun.
Marcher Morty plays his tuba.
Foom-fibba-fum!
Bam! goes the buggy
straight through the drum!
Bobby, smiling sweetly,
sucks his little thumb.

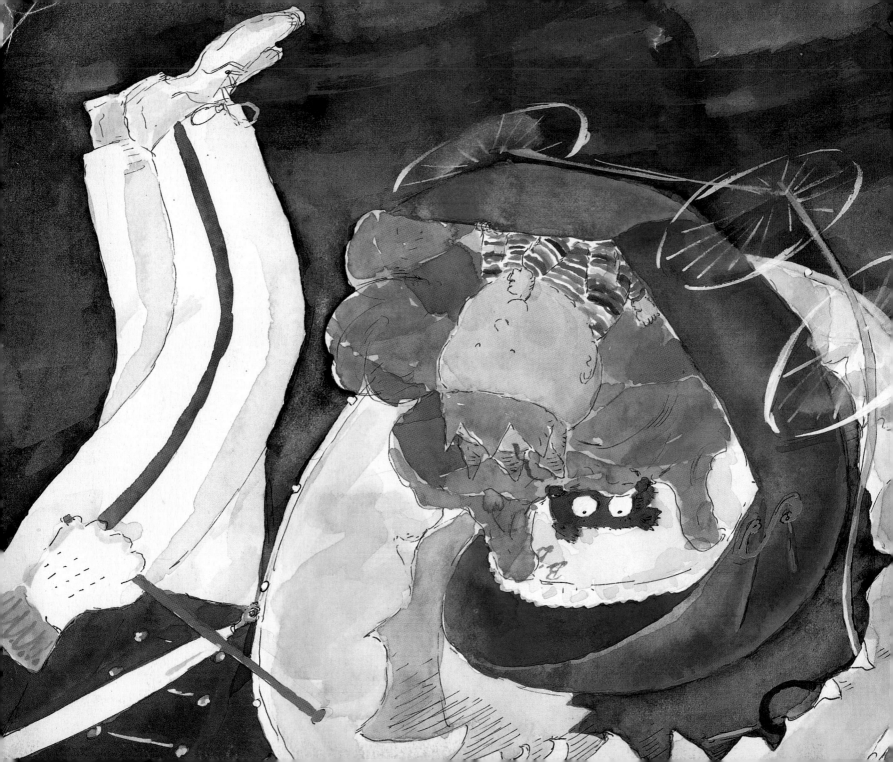

Giggling baby Bobby
sings a silly song.
The buggy's on the footbridge,
the whole town tags along.
"No! No!" squeals Bobby.
Splash! Look who's in the pond!

Here comes the playground.
"Out!" Bobby demands.
Buggy hits a stump—Wheeee!
Where will Bobby land?
The seesaw? The slide?

Whew! Softly in the sand!

Little baby Bobby
lives on a hill.
Oopsa! Oopsa!
He never sits still.
Happy-clap! goes Bobby.
Huffy-puff! goes Britta.
Rolly-strolly! goes the buggy
slowly up the hill!